RAIN AFTER MIDNIGHT

DON SKILES

Pelekinesis

Rain After Midnight by Don Skiles

ISBN: 978-1-938349-48-5
eISBN: 978-1-938349-66-9
Library of Congress Control Number: 2017931727

Sumi Ink Drawing: Marian Schell
Photograph of drawing by: Craig Kolb
Layout and Book Design by Mark Givens

First Pelekinesis Printing 2017

For information:
Pelekinesis
112 Harvard Ave #65
Claremont, CA 91711 USA

www.pelekinesis.com

RAIN AFTER MIDNIGHT

by

Don Skiles

PRAISE FOR DON SKILES

"Don Skiles' imaginative and thoughtful ruminations on urban pasts and present day complications fulfills Jack Kerouac's prescription for 'literature as companionship,' leaving you exhilarated and filled with the recognition that we're all in this together. A great book by one of my favorite writers."

—Peter Case, musician and songwriter

"Don Skiles' collection of short fiction, *Rain After Midnight*, ranges broadly across time and place to give us flashes of a life lived in different landscapes—England, western Pennsylvania, San Francisco—all the while offering us aperçus about literature and culture, memory and youth, until word by word, sentence by sentence, the collection becomes nothing less than a vital history of how a self is made, a vade mecum of how a writer comes to be."

—Gregory Djanikian

"Don Skiles is one of my favorite writers, and I love these funny, poignant, absurd and beautiful stories. I wouldn't be surprised if a little bit of Richard Brautigan lurks in the DNA of this collection."

—Elizabeth McKenzie, author of *The Portable Veblen*

For Marian

CONTENTS

SMALL TOWN

So long ago. Sitting in the attic of that grey wooden frame house in the town by the river –it was already "old" then –smoking Old Gold Straights, typing on a green portable Smith-Corona. Clack-clack-clack, eye squinted against the smoke curling up from the cigarette in the mouth. Sweat down the back; it was hot in the summer attic.

A first novel. Seventeen years old. There probably wasn't another person in that small town on the Allegheny River working on a novel. People worked in factories, mills, foundries, on the railroad, on the farm. They lost fingers, got ruptured, threw their backs out, became alcoholics.

Who wrote novels?

ROUGH CUT

Two bands from Seattle. Actually, Bellingham. *King Salmon* and *French Hip.* Caught them once on a multi-bill in Berkeley at *Freight & Salvage* with two Alaskan groups, *Deadhorse* and *Coldfoot.* Another group, *Blind Nomads,* was a no-show; never appeared. So at the last moment, a San Francisco outfit, *Lead Pipe,* got added. Quite a night, reminded me of the old days at Steppenwolf, now long gone.

King Salmon could've attained more prominence, probably. They had the rolling, rocking ride of a really solid blues group, very much like *Canned Heat.* But they had no "Bear", and no one writing better than just average songs. Maybe, in the way of things, they lacked ambition, lacked that mysterious cohesion. Start-ups suffer from the same syndrome, don't they? They unwind, lose cohesion. Out of the proverbial one hundred, how many will make IPO?

But the place had a mixologist with tattoos he'd had done in the Philippines, both arms; house-infused drinks. Great burgers. Always saves the day ... They all had a story to tell, and *French Hip* sang one they called "The Night It Snowed in Berlin".

And walking back home that night, I came on a fading inscription, cut into the sidewalk pavement, there underneath the street light. It read "Ke*ep It Real*".

SUPER EIGHT

It could never be like this again. Somehow I knew that. Back when the days all seemed like mornings. I got up and sat drinking coffee, just watching the lemon sunlight of early June flood the living room floor, while the long, white, soft curtains stirred in a fresh summer breeze.

I was going out to shoot, with a *GAF-8*, some color Super-Eight film. Hand-held, walking down the boulevard – there weren't any of those where I was, a small-sized city in north-central Pennsylvania, where they sent talented high school football players from the inner city to keep them out of harm's way.

I had a plot, of sorts, for the film, but what I really wanted was the exuberance of film. The kind of thing Truffaut and Godard captured, the famous shots of the youth running through the *Louvre*, the streets of Paris, which belonged to them. I wanted to show the moments belonging to youth, which don't come again, even though you think that of course they will.

For that, the essential was a beautiful girl – not a woman, so much, but a girl just on the cusp. I had found her, coming out of a shoe store on the main street of the town. My friend Jim, (who was working as my mentor, really, though he did not know it and neither did I) and I were sitting in a small coffee shop, at the counter, across the street. He saw her first, and pointed.

"Look at that! Can you believe it? In this town?" He touched my arm. "Wait a minute – it looks like she's with her mother." He shook his head. "My God! She looks like – what was her name – Byron's mistress?"

Byron's mistress –Teresa Guiccioli, something like that. Of course, he had many, Lord Byron. He might have been more attached to his Newfoundland dog, though, or the bear he kept at Trinity College in Cambridge.

What to say? "Will you be in my film? I know

you don't know me, but you will be perfect, I saw you come out of the shoe store over there..." I did not say any of those things. I don't remember what I said, but the mother somehow did not fear me, and the girl seemed amused, but also obviously pleased.

I wanted to outline the story to her, and met her in the college coffee café, a safe bet, to do this. For some reason, it reminded me of another meeting, years earlier, in the Snack Bar on an air base in England, with the daughter of a Master Sergeant. She had real china-blue eyes. Sitting across from her, at a scarred formica table in that drafty place, her eyes stunned me. I have never seen eyes that blue, before or since. As for the old sergeant, waving a .45, he had driven off prior young men who arrived at the door of their house.

"What's your story about?" she had asked me, leaning forward a bit. The coffee in the Snack Bar was terrible – there was no good coffee in England, at least not publicly for sale. The girl's skin was so fine-textured I thought I was seeing things.

"About? Well...it's not really about....you know, it's about Youth." I nodded, and reached for my coffee. "Yes."

"Youth?" she said, and blinked, then looked down.

I looked desperately around the Snack Bar, and took a deep breath.

KNIGHT OF THE CINEMA

Shooting film was a revelation. Even an epiphany. Everything looked different with that camera in hand, and everything looked different afterwards, too - at least for a while, as it did when you came out of a really good film, and were quiet.

And seeing what you'd got, at the end of the day; there weren't many things to do in life that could be better, more satisfying. Although he was only a young man, he felt married to the cinema when he was shooting. Looking for shots was just as good – the young girl with the black *I Love Paris* tee-shirt in the ice cream place, things like that.

It was hard to imagine getting paid to do it,

as a *profession.* What knowledge he did have of the business of film-making made him realize he could never be a director, at least not of commercial films. The making of a two-hour commercial film – and even more, getting it released, shown in theaters – was a torturous, expensive, Byzantinesque labor requiring a nerveless psychological make-up, boundless stamina, street smarts, and much, much more of a director. Sam Peckinpah had famously said that to get a film made "You have to eat a lot of shit." The phantom producer – quick, name just two – shouldered a lot of this Sisyphean load. Even so, how *did* one learn the craft?

But if you could commit to it, shooting film, creating pictures had to be a full life. You would have to be a knight of the cinema, swear fealty to the magic of those images you might capture. That could tell stories you did not even realize until you saw them together.

He had shown a very beautiful girl, one early autumn afternoon, the short film he was making. The two of them, alone together.

"That's it..." he'd said lamely after the six or

seven minutes of film.

"You're into it, aren't you?" She was looking closely at him. "Really into it, I mean."

He nodded, swallowed. "Yes. I am. I have no idea how to continue, either. How you do it, you know? Make films?"

She smiled. She was putting on a light, short, bright blue jacket she'd worn. "Don't worry. You're lucky. Believe me."

After she left, he stood in the curved bay window space, looking out at the late afternoon street, the big still-green trees moving in a slight breeze, and wondered if he was.

TELEVISION

The girl with the unbelievable smooth tawny knees would speak of what she'd watched on television, late at night. Since he never watched tv, those flickering, modern firelight reflections, and didn't own one, nor even want one, this was a problem. It seemed everyone, everyone in California, the whole country, watched television, except him... One morning, over coffee in the snack bar/café, she described a particular film, *Lord Love A Duck*, she'd seen late the previous night. (Actually, he thought, it must've been early that morning.)

"Did you see it?" she asked.

He nodded.

"Wasn't it crazy? I mean, it was – I've never seen a movie like that. What did you think it was about?"

"Very modern. California..."

She nodded vigorously.

NORWEGIAN WOOD

That afternoon, wearing a plaid lumber-jack shirt, faded tight jeans, she climbed up the ladder on a blue *Norfolk Southern* freight car, and waved; we got that sequence. With the big sun behind her like a halo of gorgeous spokes. I guess it was clear to me at least, that in the film she really wasn't real, but the Dream Girl, or even the deeper-level Jungian *anima.* The narrative line was the young men running through the town looking for her; there were glimpses, tantalizing, here and there – in a passing car, the train shots, the Library; the River Walk with the trees moving in a breeze, sitting at a café, walking down, away, in a side street, turning a corner. In a room in a large, empty house, with curtains blowing in the soft breeze.

She was a beautiful 19-year old American girl, and she would never be that beautiful again, and that was part of it, too. She'd get fat in her thirties – maybe not too much, though. Buxom. I had no idea what to do with her, outside of shooting the film, which I had persuaded her mother, seeing her walk out of a shoe store downtown, to let me do. Her father was wealthy (new money); she rode horses, and went to some college in the South that had a "party" reputation. She asked me early on to go riding with her, and I had to tell her I didn't know how to ride a horse. As Daisy said to Gatsby "Rich girls don't marry poor boys."

One hot early July day we shot a great Truffaut-like sequence, the young dudes, hair flying, running breakneck down the steep stone steps of the Library. Bursting out through those big doors. It was a great shoot.

But the assistant, my best friend, hadn't loaded any film that morning in the camera. And I hadn't checked.

SUMI INK DRAWING

"If it was all in the script, why make the film?"

– Nicholas Ray

When we got outside, a light rain was starting to fall. Earlier, it had been a thick, grey swirling fog-mist. Tree tops floated. Serene, green, peaceful, Japanese. The *koan* solved.

The streets were wet, darkness falling, quickly now, and we decided to go looking for the Chinaman (although you can't say that anymore). We never found him, but it was the idea that drove us.

Were we young?

What of History? Or, history, with the little h. Of the man of "sub-par mental abilities", who lived on the streets of Mexico City for over three months eating garbage, what is to be said? Or of the leper in Calcutta, a woman, with maggots in an ulcer on her hip? What is to be said? If you're looking for a story with some deeper significance, this is probably not the one. Still and all, it happened, and (as they say) it's good to tell it.

ON FOOT

The brigade is gone now. Long gone. The foot messengers, who worked out of the first floor in the Hearst Building, at the busy intersection of Third Street ("Three Street"), and Market Street, in San Francisco.

But he remembered it well. So it was not gone. Not at all. They were indeed a happy few.

He and Harris Gale – "Harry" – were by far the youngest, in their early twenties. Both of them were students at San Francisco State, the *plus ultra* of urban collegiate life. The messengers worked from one to seven weekdays, and eight to two Saturdays, a perfect schedule for a full-time student. It was do-able, although he often thought of what he'd be capable of in his classes if he wasn't working that many hours a week. But that paycheck every Monday was essential.

Besides, it was a good training in real-life journalism, which he'd considered majoring in. It was a school, a college, in itself.

"Somebody should make a movie of this place," Bert, the uniformed, dapper short elevator operator said as he pulled the wire screen closed on the old, ornate elevator. "I'm tellin' you..."

Bert at some point in his life had most likely been in the military. His small shoes –black oxfords –had tips buffed to a true mirror shine. You *could* see yourself in those shoe tips, and he'd point this out.

"Spit shine," he said. "You young guys don't know how to do it, either." He would shake his head.

Bert was old – at least as old as the rest of the messenger brigade. There was George, who was himself a dapper dresser, always wearing a trim sports coat, and a grey fedora, rarely seen anymore. He was said to be in his seventies, but he was in good physical shape, quite up to a "long run", down to the Ferry Building or over to the far end of Montgomery, where it ran into Columbus – nearly North Beach. He was a retired motorman who'd run streetcars (on Market Street) most of his career – the whole lot of them; the J Church, the K Ingleside, the L Taraval, the M Ocean View. "Yep . .. all the way out. To the Zoo, to City College."

Marvin was a short, messy man, the opposite of neat, trim George. Marvin always sought the short runs – a few blocks – and invariably stopped en route "to grab a coffee," and check his bets. He really belonged out at Bay Meadows, or Golden Gate Fields, but had never gotten it together for that life. On his days off he rode the train to Bay Meadows – "Heaven!", he termed it. "And the train lets you off right in front there! Right across the street! You can't beat that."

Marvin never seemed to win at his various ventures, but he was always hopeful, and would talk of what he would do if he ever "made a big score." He favored retiring to Hawaii, a place he'd seen while in the Army.

Leon was the third – he was younger than George or Marvin. Maybe his late fifties. His past was checkered, a word he used, and the other messengers said he'd gone to UC Berkeley as a young man. He had many interests, and always carried a book, reading it while he waited for his next run assignment. He was also a very good chess player.

The thing about Leon was that he believed there were people on other planets. Especially Venus, for some reason. He claimed to have visited them in his dreams or some kind of waking vision; he was unclear. But certain of it.

He also claimed the *kahunas* of Hawaii possessed arcane, esoteric knowledge lost to Westerners. They had been known to bring the dead back to life, for one thing. This was a fact. But they themselves were dying out, their ancient knowledge not being passed on, except in a few rare cases. Leon claimed many ancient peoples' knowledge was now gone, lost, and this was what screwed up the world, put it in the condition it was in. It had not always been so; in fact, this was a recent phenomenon. Rather than evolution, there was devolution. As an example, he pointed to the *Egyptian Book of the Dead*, which he had a copy of, saying that it had to be obvious that those who prepared the mummies had knowledge no longer accessible, powerful practices and rituals lost. And there were many other similar examples. You didn't need a PhD to know these things.

The most colorful of the group was Joe, the motorcycle messenger. He was, in the words of the other men, "Simple – you know what I mean?" Some said he'd been a promising boxer until he took a bad beating.

Joe was physically strong, and in his leathers, which he was always in, astride the cycle, his "hog", a Harley with a sidecar that held all manner of materials he was transporting, Joe was poetic. The main problem was that Joe was easily distracted.

"Whatever happens in life, it won't be what you expect," Marvin said, looking at Joe astride his machine one day out in Jessie Street, a dirty, dreary, dark alley running behind the Hearst Building, where winos slept and a flickering neon sign advertised the Jessie Hotel, a notorious flop house where you could spend the night for a dollar. A famous story the reporters on the City Desk still discussed was that of a bum found dead in his bed in the Jessie Hotel. Eighty thousand dollars had been found stuffed in the mattress.

Jessie Street shuddered, because the giant presses that printed the newspaper ran beneath it, and when an edition was run, things moved above. The pressmen, a proud fraternity, stood out in the alley smoking, wearing their odd military-like hats made of newspaper. Nobody else wore these. The typesetters, up above on the third and fourth floors, wore green visors, like dealers in a casino, and had to learn to read upside down. If for some reason they took offense, a reporter's story could appear without its concluding paragraph, or with embarrassing, glaring spelling confusions.

So the foot messengers were yet another fraternity in the business, as even the reporters – the journalists – were. But there were few of them, and they were somehow a breed apart, unique.

In Jessie Street, some young toughs set a

bum, a wino, on fire. The reporters discussed it for a while.

"They used to give a guy a hot foot."

"Times have changed, eh? Now, they set you on fire. Like those monks, over in Vietnam. But they do it to themselves."

"Immolation. Can you imagine? You smell those gasoline fumes. Then, a flick of a Zippo. Whoosh!" The reporter threw his hands up.

Joe, the motorcycle messenger, was detained in the White House department store; police were called, and Nichols, the Night Editor, a man who looked straight from Central Casting for the part of a night editor, had to vouch for Joe to get him released. The White House was the last run of the day, and the final copy was often not ready until near 7:30. Joe, waiting, had wandered off into a floor display of furniture, laid down on a sofa, and fell asleep. When he woke, the Advertising people were gone, the store was darkened. Joe looked out a window, was seen by people passing in the street, whom he gestured to. The rest followed.

The messengers ate their lunch back behind

the first floor Display Ad office and counter, in a seldom used room, paneled in wood. Nobody seemed to know what it was for, or who'd occupied it. He and Harry used it often. Nobody bothered you in there.

" The real old days," Harry said, eating a bunch of green grapes, which he loved, one by one. He looked around. "Hearst himself could've been in here. What do you think?"

"Could be...makes you think. What –who– will be here in a hundred years from now? For instance."

Harry grinned, a grape poised between two fingers.

"You fucking English majors," he said, and popped the grape into his mouth.

THE STRAILEY BUILDING IRREGULARS

CRANE SHOT: Drops down, moving over what is clearly a small college campus, lush in mid-summer.

We come in tighter, on a two-story frame house, sitting near the corner of a narrow, obviously old street - Strailey Street, a street sign reads. The house is wood, painted a soft grey with white trim. Probably early 20th century.

We come smoothly in and look in a second story window. It's a faculty office, with three desks, somewhat crowded. The desk nearest the window is neat; a row of books is held at the head of it by two small book-ends, small brass lions. A few manila file folders in a small stack neatly on one side.

The second desk, facing the first one, is the reverse. Papers are haphazardly heaped on top of it with a few obviously fallen off the side onto the floor. One drawer yawns open, and there is a pair of dirty, grass-stained sneakers, which we can almost smell, sitting on the desk chair. A scuffed brown briefcase, partially open, sits precariously on the side of the desk. We see a small plaque on this desk, which reads "Strailey Building Irregulars".

The third desk takes up more space, and fits into the other half of the room. The chair is an executive-type high-backed black recliner. There is a glass plate over the work area of this desk, and there are several tastefully framed photos at one end. There is a tennis racket in one corner near the desk, with a shiny, black and white tube of balls on which we can clearly see *Wilson*.

THE CAMERA now pans smoothly past the desks, out the open wooden frame office door, into a narrow high-ceilinged hall, and we follow it down, left, to the end of the hall, where another office door stands open.

Two desks here, both facing the door, with ample room between; a sort of small path space. Both these desks look older, worn wood dark black. Small piles of books stacked on each. There is a carpet on the floor of this room, with a geometric design of circles. One desk has a green, upholstered and obviously well-used wing-backed chair in front and to one side of it.

Conspicuous on the one side of the other desk is what looks like a coiled rope ladder, lying directly under a window, which is cracked open with an old-fashioned screen insert. Some papers on the closer desk lift and rustle; there's a slight, soft summer breeze, and we also see the thick dark green foliage moving slowly on a large tree outside. White, thin curtains move very slightly in the window frames.

There is a dart board on the opposing wall at the end of the small "path" between the two desks, with several metal-headed darts in it. It contains a photograph-portrait of former Vice President Spiro Agnew, which the camera now closes in on, as *music comes up.*

LATE INTO
AUTUMN NIGHTS
AT A SMALL BAR

There was a guy who was a chef. Frederick. Wore a black eye patch, even though he was still young. Always sat way down at the curved end of the long, long bar, a piece of art that bar, fine worked wood, you could not find one easily now. The bar of railroad men. Serious.

It was that place. We drank, and talked. Avicenna. Boethius' *Consolation of Philosophy*. Augustine, Chaucer, *Gawain and the Green Knight*.

Then, an effortless *segue* to Godard, Fellini, Sam Peckinpah, Dennis Hopper. And the Russians – long films of the war, the horrors of the Pripet Marshes, Stalingrad. Paulus and the Sixth Army, trapped. Lacan's lectures on anxiety. Louis Malle's *My Dinner with Andre.*

One night, into November, we came out, it was snowing, and we had been drinking tequila. Tequila and snow. How long had we talked? No e-mail, no blogs, no posts, no texts.

That was the night a young guy, in his white tee-shirt, threw a whiskey bottle completely over a three-story building, next door.

Incredible.

SOMETHING ELSE

It was a novel that would be read in the future. Holding the trim hard-cover edition, it could already be seen as a well-designed paperback, in the hands of students, in college quads, neat rimmed green squares with benches, where maple leaves fell in brilliant profusion in autumn. Tucked in white bookshelves in tidy dorm rooms where sun moved over the soft wood floor; in clean and dirty book bags, backpacks; carried on the subway, read on small screens during the long commutes in big, black-liveried luxury motor coaches, carrying the young wizards of Google and Facebook and Apple, to Cupertino, Sunnyvale, Menlo Park.

It would be sold then, pass through many sets of page-turning hands, the pages themselves succumbing, crumbling, some torn, folded, the famous dog-eared, now shoved into a shelf in a used book store in San Francisco, another one in Berkeley, a third, in London. It would acquire marginalia, cryptoisms, underlinings, exhortations, exclamation points, three in a row.

It would be thrown in the gray waste basket beside the battered, scarred desk of the Night Editor at a large metropolitan daily, who actually thought you threw away paperbacks after reading them. So he told the copy boy who fished it out.

In its own inscrutability, it would initiate unimaginable connections, thoughts, dreams. It would enter neurological pathways at blinding speed, and propagate in cyberspaces, even as it was shredded, pulped, for something else.

Something else.

TRAIN

The train would go up the other side of the river in the night, the whistle something oddly comforting. "The Midnight Bummer." Why it was called that, no one ever said. Maybe you could bum a ride if the conductor, on his last run, was friendly. Nod and smile. "Seem to have misplaced my ticket..." Searching pockets.

The train hauled whiskey from the big Schenley Distillery five miles up the Allegheny River. He had never seen it, but imagined it many times. A worker fell one night and drowned in one of the huge vats, 212 gallons, they said. "You can't swim in it..." The inevitable joke about being well-pickled. The story resembled that one of the worker at the brickyard, hauled into the big kiln by a conveyor belt.

It was one of those nights, especially the long, hot, soft-drink – Virginia Dare, 7-Up, Nehi Grape – quiet summer nights, when it may have been he started dreaming, wide-awake, of being a writer. Without any clear notion or model of what it meant, but a sense, somewhere, that it was like the midnight train, the echoing midnight urgent fading whistle, going up the steep valley in the soft darkness. You heard that, but even more, you felt it.

He was sure of that, but didn't know how to tell anyone.

THE 500,000 APPS

He told me, later, among many other confidences, that he'd started drinking heavily when he worked on the railroad. "It was part of the ethos," he said. "You know what I mean? Railroaders drink." He drank riding high up in the caboose, and was fired.

He progressed. Drinking alone, late into the night; his "visitations." Sometimes, defying the Fates, he got in his white Corvair and drove to sites. Places where he'd suffered, or passed some time, or knew some happiness. Even places he remembered throwing up, like at the foot of Hyde Street, across from The Buena Vista, while the cable car clanked, and the grip man rang the bell, leading him to muse on this being a San Francisco Hell, the cable car and grip man replacing Charon and his boat. There'd been a girl, a British girl, who worked in the BV and that figured in. But she married a BOAC pilot.

Another was the lush front of "The Captain's House." This was a fantastical Victorian, on Douglass Street, built in 1892 by an Irish clipper captain. Glass brought from Venice. Redwood, from right over in Mill Valley. A turret apartment, where he never penetrated physically, but imagined many times.

There was The Trident, over in Sausalito. The late afternoon jazz jam sessions (now faded into the bright air above the rippling waters) starting at four, let you get buzzed pleasantly while soaking in the music like the sun. Pitchers of citrusy margaritas; some scrambled eggs, muffin/jam for the stomach. By eight or so, you could segue over to The Tides bookstore, and lose yourself. Or talk to Betsy, who ran the place and knew everything, from Jung and Anaïs Nin's works, to the esoterica of the *Tarot* and Edgar Cayce. Nostradamus. *The Master and Margarita, Dr. Zhivago.* Giulietta Masina, Fellini's wife/muse (especially in *The Nights of Cabiria).* Tantric sex. She married a

Shakespearean actor, who had a day job as a gardener and moved to Santa Fe.

The sacred portal of cinema. Out at The Surf, smelling of kelp, iodine, salt, espresso and popcorn. The Music Hall, where *Sundays and Cybele* had left him, blinded with tears, suddenly out on Larkin Street, people walking around him. Saint Cinema.

And the old industrial loft space, sacred it was, Number One Enterprise Street, next to the commercial bakery. No elevator. A feat to get into it, ascend a grimy, slippery metal ladder, then hoist up onto a floor depression, feet dangling. Eight-foot long sink, and the tall neon *Falstaff Beer* sign glass, on top of the brewery, by the freeway. Filling, re-filling, filling, mesmeric, robotic. All night long till the dawn. Spread out to the east like a magic carpet was the twinkling city of Ambrose Bierce, Twain, Jack London, Jack Kerouac. The writing on the far wall of that big space (before it was fashionable): *I'm taking to the highway. On the road. I'm gone.*

He should have stayed there.

ALGORITHMS

Took to shaving his head, wearing a dark blue robe with carp printed on it, that he bought in Japantown, "Nihonmachi", drinking green tea, burning incense, reading haiku and the classic Japanese poets in early morning. And the remarkable *Essays in Idleness*, the *Tsurezuregusa*, of the 14th century monk, Kenkō.

Writing of scrolls, Kenkō advises "Imperfect sets are better."

COMING THROUGH THE CITY

Sat in his capacious cream white robe, somewhat like Balzac's monk's habit, by the fire, read late into the night. Even to two, sometimes. At that hour, it was quiet, finally. Drank a tot or two of *Jameson's*. If there was a storm, wind knocking the windows, later the lashings, hissings, rattlings of hard rain, even better. A time to think of books - Robert Burton, Jeremy Taylor, Izaak Walton – read in college long ago, friends now long, long gone, not seen for many years. Yet their faces, and voices, came easily. Where were they, where had they ended up? But in the unusual instance when such a person actually appeared, coming through the city (for old time's sake, even), there turned out to be little to say. A whole life had intervened. A lifetime.

One thing was clear. They – most, at least, not all – had not done what they were expected to. They had deconstructed, "done something different." The great fear, the *tsunami* of conformity, convention, the ordinary; the tight (usually white) collar, the thirty-year mortgage box house with a little square lawn, the robot trance in an office cubicle – these had been avoided.

They were different. Nobody knew what to make of it, even now. But it wasn't what was expected. No.

FAMOUS BOOK STORE

Wet streets glisten, glitter, in the street lights' glare. The wind in off the Pacific is gusting hard tonight, and I linger in the famous book store. Richard Brautigan's novel *Trout Fishing In America* ends with the word *mayonnaise*, because he always wanted to end a novel with that word. Across Columbus, Broadway, the Condor Club sign winks on, off, on, off, and you can hear snatches of the barker's rap over here.

It is the end of the year, and I feel knotted, empty inside. Many do, I believe. No one knows what the new year will bring, although some believe they do. They have made plans. I have no plan, other than (maybe) getting coffee down the street, or going across to Specs, but it is too.

unreal for the likes of me, Specs is. It is the small Duchy of Unbelief in there, of which I am not a citizen.

Among the ranks of books shelved, waiting, here in the famous bookstore, is where I feel at home. Even at peace. All would be well if the world was a bookstore, like this one. Nothing terrible can happen here, and I always linger.

Some author on television said they'd read a novel of Dickens four times. I wonder if that's possible, or true. Each time you read something like Dickens, it's different. Even the first sentence, that all-important, pregnant first one, is different. If it's been long enough, you can't remember reading it. Or, more interesting, *where* you read it.

I ran out of funds one winter in the Lake Country in England. Found myself in a sort of large old cottage up there, on a bitter cold night, and I was down by the large fireplace, which really did heat (nearly) the entire room, and no light except a small, old reading lamp with a wonderful mica shade, a Victorian sort of lamp, casting a small, soft pool of light on

the book (Coleridge) I was reading. My hosts
were an American professor of Romantic Literature at Purdue University, and his young wife.
They had a two-year old boy, Jason. Christy,
the prof, was on sabbatical, or maybe it was
half-sabbatical. I met them in a local pub, The
Green Man, told them my story, they took me in
until I could get things straightened out. I tried
to stay out of the way as best I could. It was the
end of that year, too, and when I was in funds
again I bought a stout pair of really good boots,
and caught the British Rail to London, early
one frosty morning, feeling I should stay there,
wanting to stay. But not able to stay. There was
no one else in the small station. Just me.

It took me some time to get out of London,
where I lived in a small room near Kings' Cross.
When you opened the door, the first thing you
saw was yourself in a mirror on a small chest of
drawers.

When I was in the senior year of high school,
I conceived the idea of going to some port city –
New York, or New Orleans, say – and shipping
out. I wanted to get to Singapore. Why I didn't

know – something in the very name. Singapore. I tried to convince my best friend, Paul, to come with me, go with me; talked up the adventures we'd have. Half way around the world, to Singapore. But he said he couldn't do it. "I'm going to the Virginia Military Institute in the Fall, " he said. "VMI."

Now, many years later, I was standing in the doorway of the famous bookstore, my feet starting to get wet, I was hearing the rain strike the pavement with a sting, and probably somebody drove by on Columbus, looked out the car window streaked with rivulets of rain, it was the end of the year, saw me for a couple of seconds, there.

"Look at that guy. Standing there – getting out of the rain..." And I had just read that last sentence, last word. *Mayonnaise.*

GONE BOOKSTORE

He lived in an old apartment building, with peeling paint, on the corner. Many apartment buildings were on corners. Why was this?

It was going on 7pm. Turning dark, a light drizzle coming down. San Francisco was a city of rain, of drizzle, of fogs that were like drizzle. It was a bookstore night. When you lived alone, you spent a lot of evenings in bookstores.

He'd gone to this particular bookstore for thirty years, or more, now. It had begun its life as a used bookstore, back when there were a lot of them, and it was still that (having added vinyl records, CDs, even videos.) At the front of the store it offered the latest selections, the most recently published books. These what you saw when you entered past the cash register, a narrow passage (to prevent thefts); up on a raised sort of platform/dais, like some sort of minor worthy you had to pay tribute to, sat the cashier of the moment. The till.

He often traded arcane quips with this particular guy, Mike. It had become a sort of greeting ritual.

"Mike," he called, standing momentarily in the passageway. "What sort of man would wear two-toned oxfords? Black and white? Or white bucks?"

"Not you..." Mike called, sorting a stack of books in front of him carefully. "Not you..."

He nodded, sauntered slowly into the main part of the first floor. The place reminded him of shops he'd been in - many places, many nights. He used to see some of the old Beats down in the famous joint on Columbus, which he'd once heard one call a "gone place." What did the Beats mean by that? Probably it was hipster lingo, for "stoned," "out of it," transcendent to higher, deeper realms of reality. A gone cat was, to put it succinctly, enlightened. He *knew*. He had left mundanity and the endless bourgeois chicken scratch.

Albert Henry's. Stacey's. Cody's. Alexander's Books. The Jim Mate Pipe Shop ... all gone now... Thinking of them...Not like the internet, that was for sure. Nobody worried or chafed at speeds of downloads. There was no speed of browsing. Gone bookstore.

David, his friend back East, had e-mailed him that with autumn coming on, winter nearly visible, in Siberia the hunters would perform a rite of throwing a silver thimble of vodka into the fire, to wish for warmth through the coming long, long winter nights. In the same e-mail, he'd mentioned that he'd read the popular singer and movie star of the 1950s, Mario Lanza, never went anywhere without twenty thousand dollars in cash in his pocket.

Bookstores were sacred places to writers. He always found he began to think of places he'd written, the various places over years. With shirt cuffs rolled up, workmanlike. The fantastic down-at-the-heels apartment/flat on 21st Street, where somebody had built a small, narrow extension on the end of the second story, behind the tiny kitchen. It was glassed-in, with a wooden door wedged tightly at one end, a perfect desk. There was a sofa bed at the other end, where he had often sat, with the cup of coffee, and the cigarette, smoke curling up, always fine to watch, and dream.

But it was the panoramic, million-dollar view of San Francisco – especially at night, twinkling like the proverbial thousand stars – that made visitors gasp. In such a shacky, worn, run-down place it was unexpected, that view, that perspective. He'd often wondered who had built it, added it.

One night there. Sitting listening to a Bach *Cello Concerto*, wrapped in an old Pendleton blanket. Fog rolling in, spilling over Twin Peaks in a wave. Down by the Bay, the old famous horns would be croaking; further away, the muffled sounds of the surf, rolling.

It would be a cold, dark, long night. Haloes around the street lights.

THAT BOOK

I wrote most of that book when I was living in the back top third floor apartment on California Street, in the late Seventies. I wrote it on an electric typewriter (can't remember the brand) I loved. The book was published four years later, it had a modest *success d'estime*, and I have never (so far at least) published another one.

Although I have written several. The number of unpublished works in America must be staggering, mind-numbing. All those words! Sentences, paragraphs, pages. Hours upon hours upon hours, the *begats* of the fiction Biblical. The catalog is vast, long, sad. Many have enrolled in it.

I saw, today, on my halting, limping peregrinations, another place where I wrote. I was so young then...At night I would lie in a bed placed in the smooth half-circle inscribed by the bay windows, listening as the wind made the palm tree outside make its inimitable sound, a sort of soft clacking rustle, like no other sound. A sound of the desert. But I was in the city.

Who lives there now? If one were to ring the bell, inquire, say "I once lived here, a long time ago..." What would that bring? Perhaps, if the current occupant was compassionate, an invitation to come in, a drink, an asking even to tell one's story. Face to face with it all, again.

There's the Dr. Pepper plant, no longer there, that I walked around several times, in the rain, with a girl who knew I loved her. The building where another writer –and maybe even more – lived, unknown to me then, discovered years later. The sedate house where the abortionist practiced. The fern bar beloved of airline stewardesses. The house of the Satanic master, and author. The old restaurant, old then (still there). The hamburger place where the beautiful people paid outrageous prices. The Casbah bar, that had hanging, diaphanous blue curtains.

The future no one saw in those *au courant* places, just as the books one might have written remained just out of sight.

But that was no reason – no – to stop.

LATE CAREER

The writer William Saroyan lived in a house not far from this one, in the Sunset District of San Francisco. He was then at the end of his career, and maybe no longer went to the track daily, hoping for a score, and then to bars where it was always like a *fête* night. There must have been late nights when he took a cab, and looked at the wet gleam of the streets flashing, flickering by, and wondered where it had all gone – the great fame, so heady; the prizes, the easy money, the sense of never-ending pleasure readily available. The pretty girls - sitting not at, but *on* the bar at Izzy's. Always waiting.

He no longer dreamed up stories, but instead dwelt increasingly on his own private one, trying to fathom it. And what he dwelt on was, *what makes a voice authentic?*

He badly wanted to say that to the bulbous-nosed, thick-necked cabbie –where did he live, where did a cabbie live? In the Tenderloin, in a single room with a broken window, looking out on a dirty brick wall? But he didn't, instead giving him his last fiver for a tip, listening to that special sound a cab door makes when it closes on a rainy night.

THE CABIN

Reading. Reading late at night, with only the sound of the fire, and that warmth. A Franklin stove, in a cabin, North Pennsylvania. *Penn's Woods*, aptly named.

At night, I wrote, seated at a long, solid oak table made by hand by my Donegal grandfather in the late nineteenth century. No nails in it. Looking out a small four-paned window. There was electricity, but on some nights I'd light the kerosene lamps. Writing like that, in the soft light of those lamps, with only the sound of the fire glowing in the stove. That was contentment, satisfaction.

Very late, I'd step outside into the visceral sharpness of the December cold. On some nights, watch a snowfall coming down. There is a sound to snow falling at night like that, one similar to the guarantee of the sound of rain falling. Once in a while I'd walk out to the main road in it. Few things as magical, wondrous, as freshly fallen snow.

When I came to the cabin, I was looking for some space, to figure things out. I was still – barely, as it turned out – young enough to believe that might be possible. And not in the conventional ways of starting some business, or devoting my energies to "making some real money." No. I did not have those ambitions.

Down in the small town, ten miles away, I'd see a young couple occasionally, shopping for groceries, or in the local restaurant/pizza place. They had two small children, a boy and a younger girl. They seemed to have already found everything out, that couple, and those beautiful children. At the same time, I had a deep sense I would never know their type of contentment and wholeness. It was a heavy thought, and on some days, grey and somber outside, the temperature falling, I sat leaden in my chair with it, even letting the fire go out. What was to be done?

Years earlier in my life, I'd met a girl with whom I'd constructed an entire refuge fantasy (we didn't know it was called that then) where we lived in a cabin back in the woods, far back. She loved the bassist Jack Bruce, who was one – third of the power blues group Cream. In some variations of this fantasy, I wrote her letters (no e-mail "back in the day") about the cabin, and in some, thin for material, I wrote that Jack Bruce also had a cabin back in there where we were.

There was another, earlier cabin. It was the retirement house my Italian stepfather was building (but never finished) in the deer hunting woods of northwest Pennsylvania, near Cook Forest. I was taken there as a twelve and thirteen year old, legal age to hunt deer, but I turned out not to be a hunter. I had no heart for it. The life of "the camp,", where the men drank heavily from a large brown stone crock of whiskey, and yarned of eating bear steaks, then stumbled out of the uninsulated frame of the cabin to piss in the snow, didn't involve me, although I knew it was supposed to. I wanted to leave as soon as I got there.

Two years later, my stepfather suffered the first of the heart attacks. The second killed him. The house remained unfinished, and I never saw it again.

A KIND OF POETRY

There was a very long, straight tree-lined road, cutting a distinct dark line across the lush, green English countryside. Those trees – they were so evenly spaced it seemed a sort of optical illusion. At the end of this road was the great house, visible on its slight rise from a long distance away. Some wags called it Toad Hall – and in fact there was a Toad Hall over towards Fenstanton. He had heard the name Pendbury House. In World War II, it had housed some sort of super-secret Air Ministry headquarters, it was said. But it was also said it had been the ancestral home of Lord Sandwich, the inveterate gambler whose culinary invention everyone knew. It wasn't Oliver Cromwell's (the Protector) house, who'd been born in Huntingdon, nearby – where Sandwich was also from.

Part of the charm of England ("Why doesn't somebody just pull the plug, and let the whole damn island go down the drain?" GIs would carp repeatedly) was these old, old places with long, long histories. His roommate in the barracks, Steele, claimed he was related to a baron, "back there, in the fifteenth century." Steele's girlfriend in the States (which the Air Force officially called the Zone of the Interior, or ZI –or, if you'd been stationed in Germany, "the land of round doorknobs") sent him letters written on gauzy, lightly colored paper, always affixing a graphic lip-sticked kiss at the end, above her name.

"Look at *that*!" Steele would say, showing the letter page. "Will you look at that!"

Steele had been bounced around several bases in England, primarily because he was a Graphics Illustrator, and not many units had need for this specialty.

"They kept me over at Burtonwood – over there near Liverpool, big MATS base – when I first came over...then, next thing I know, they sent me to South Ruislip. If only I coulda stayed there! Right in London – there's a tube stop right there. You wear civvies, and live in a flat. Unbelievable." Steele then had been sent to what turned out to be a nearly decommissioned base, Duxbury, and then to Mildenhall, before finally coming to rest at Alconbury.

He wondered if Steele's story of "the baron" was true, or family legend. Laying in his bunk at night in the barracks, listening to what did seem like near-endless rain hitting the old building , and Steele's steady snoring, the litany of airbases – so many, on such a small island – rolled through his head. *Bentwaters. Brize Norton. Bruntingthorpe. Chelveston. Lakenheath.. Molesworth, Northolt...*

They were a kind of poetry, like Samarkand, Timbuktu, Smolensk, Aleppo, Fez.

EARLY AUTUMN

Some early autumn rain, with the change in the sky of grey-black clouds sailing, ponderous, or light, in long line, white-greys.

Thinking of a party, at Jerry Harris's, one evening. There were lights throughout a small woods, right behind his home, and people moved among the trees and the glow of the lights. You could hear voices, laughter; somewhere in the house, the music of the time – the Beatles, the Incredible String Band, Iron Butterfly. Joe Cocker. Dylan, rasping away. The MJQ.

A softness, a fine gossamer, in the evening air, even in the deep black overhead, where myriad bright stars gathered. The whole burst of the Milky Way. Jerry's place was "out in the country." But not too far. Just right.

His house was a rambling arts and crafts style, green and white. Small rooms, the kitchen the largest room. The house had a rumpled comfortableness, a well-lived in feel. Not decorator-style.

You might remember it thirty years later at a party in Pismo Beach, where small Chinese lanterns were strung, and a dragon appeared. You might meet the girl you would marry on a night like this.

What I wanted to do was sit and listen to the autumn rain. I'd always liked the sound of rain, even if I had to go out in it. But I loved sitting listening to a steady rain, or a light one, maybe drinking a good cup of coffee, with a liqueur. If there was a fire crackling in the fireplace, logs on an andiron, all the better. That sound.

You could be back in England, even back in the early 19th century. Coleridge, Wordsworth. Before the railways and the full force of the Industrial Revolution, when people routinely walked ten miles, or more, daily.

Ten miles.

FULKE GREVILLE

The old Nissen hut sat not far off the end of the long, long runway that had been put in early in WWII, so heavy bombers could use the base. Now sleek supersonic jets veered up off it, shaking the ancient roof of the hut (which had housed German POWs once), the same roof where the large English water rats ran at night, waking them as they tried to sleep in this improvised barracks.

Grissom, an old Staff sergeant who had no upper teeth, said, pointing upward, "I tell ya, one a these nights when the fog's in, one of them suckers gonna come right in here and do all of us."

In this unlikely space, he read, sitting on his bunk near the glowing belly of an M41 stove. All manner of things – Heraclitus, Pliny, the

Pre-Socratics in a red, paperback volume he bought in Heffer's bookshop in Cambridge. *The Outsider*, Colin Wilson's famous best-seller, that he wrote living in a sleeping bag on Hampstead Heath.

In Cambridge, which was only 19 miles away, he'd read in the coffee places – the Kenya, the Guild - and then walk around the old university town, carrying his book. He'd walked down to the large inner quad of King's College, right on Trumpington Street, after a 4/6 spaghetti dinner – *spag bol* – that filled, warmed him. There he'd stood, in the dark November chill coming up off the Cam (it was really the Ouse, but was called the Cam in Cambridge, just as the Thames was called the Isis in Oxford) on the crunching gravel path under a lighted window – you could see the firelight from a fireplace flickering, pulsing – and listened to somebody playing a harpsichord in the rooms. It was something hard to imagine, the life of such a place where the students had fireplaces in their rooms and played the harpsichord.

"She plays on the *viola di gamba...*" his friend Charley had quipped once, in his South Carolina drawl. "Vivaldi with his red beard, and all those nuns, sawing away at their instruments!" He made the motions of frenetic sawing with a violin bow, laughing softly, shaking his head. Charley was an Auto Pilot Repair Specialist, and had told him, among other things, the story of Fulke Greville, an English poet who was also the life-long friend of Sir Philip Sidney, the great model figure of the English Renaissance period. The thing about this story was that they had met the first day of school, and remained close friends after that, until Sidney's untimely, early death.

There were the books, too, that they'd read punting down the Cam, through the lovely Backs, just like students. Who'd know the difference? Ben Hecht, some chronicle of Cerberus, the many-headed dog of Hell, while floating under the Bridge of Sighs, modeled after the one in Venice. Pulling up under a willow on the bank, drinking six shilling wine, and reading lines alternatively, from Marlowe, Shakespeare. Coleridge's *Rime of the Ancient Mariner*, and the poems of John Donne, and other Metaphysicals, while a long, distended condom floated slowly by the punt. Blake, and talking about Samuel Palmer, whose fantastic, small paintings, which glowed, were in an exhibit at the Fitzwilliam.

There were other things, too. The English girl, whose legs went on forever, in The Eagle, a 17th century pub, on the ceiling of which were inscribed, written by them, the names and nicknames of WWII air crews. "It's all that bicycling. The legs." Pendarvus, a friend of Charley's, also from South Carolina, said, smoking a Dunhill briar pipe, like a don, with an Earl of St. Andrews' Burberry scarf thrown stylishly round his throat.

And there was the phone number, written slantingly on the fly leaf of a paperback Penguin edition of Gerard Manley Hopkins' poetry, by another English girl, Patricia, he'd met in the red double-decker bus rocking and rolling slowly through the Fen Country towards Peterborough.

"An American. In the Air Force. Reading Hopkins..." She had smiled, as she wrote down her phone number.

DEEP HOUSE

The big red Leyland double-decker bus was waiting, there in the old village square, where there was a WWI memorial monument, a tea shoppe, a "chippy" – a fish n' chips place, a very good one. The early summer night was soft, the air coming from miles of open fields, in every direction. It was East Anglia, an old part of an old country. Ely Cathedral was not far off, and although the big red bus spewed heavy diesel fumes, and idled loudly, the village itself – the village – seemed rooted in the spot, quiet, very old.

It was difficult to relate in words. But you could feel it, and so much more. When you left the square, sitting in the swaying upper deck, you'd had fish n' chips, your fingers smelt of malt vinegar and had newspaper print traces on them you noticed as you lit a rich Pall Mall. Deeper, you had the village, receding behind you, a soft smudge of yellow lights. It would be there the next time, the one after that, too. It would be there, it had always been there, and it remained.

Memory, memory.

FOG

That was the year of sitting. Listening to the fog horns, which often began at mid-day, and by evening, with the fog thick outside, wrapping the house like a blanket, the steady crackle, soft glow, of the Franklin Stove, that reliably drove all before it.

The fog was salt fog, a thousand feet high, right in off the massive Pacific, often covering the entire coast, It reminded him, as he sat in the gentle old rocker, hoping the phone would not ring, of the dense, cold, heavy fogs of East Anglia – the flat, marshy Fen Country – in England. Walking in Cambridge, with a heavy woolen scarf wrapped to his chin, this fog penetrated, chilled to the bone. Down by the river, in the Backs behind the famous colleges, it was a ghostly, floating world.

And in London, although the fogs were no

longer legendary and lethal, you could see little in front of you. Sounds emerged, became vital. It was not hard to imagine Sherlock Holmes, in his cape and deerstalker, would suddenly appear. It swirled around lamp posts, and down into the Underground stations, the Tube – Shadwell → Limehouse → Westferry → Poplar → Blackwall → East India.

On the base, everything became still. The Wing Commander, Colonel Foster, became lost out on a runway in his favorite jeep, and ran into one of the aircraft. Men, armed, were dispersed to secure the perimeter, sheep emerged from the fog, while the men, teeth chattering, wondered, for a mad few seconds, if indeed the Russian saboteurs, so long warned of, had come. Had WWIII finally begun?

Walking with Charley on the road that ran by the base, he realized he could hear him, but not see him. He stuck his arm out straight. "Look at that," he said. "You can't see your hand in front of your face." The famous saying was true.

All this – and much, much more – in memory, years later. But quite, quite visible.

ENGLISH OAKS

There had been some majestic English oaks, off the far, far end of the main runway of the airbase I was stationed on for three years in the Air Force. An old area of England - but everything in England was old, and you came to understand that - known as Alconbury Hill. In the spring especially, when they started to turn to shades of green, the oaks were a wonder.

I could stand at one of the windows in the Quonset hut we were barracked in, and watch them move grandly in the winds sweeping down over East Anglia from the North Sea. A stately contrast to the wickedly sleek jets streaking up off the long runway into the Constable skies of big clouds and blue deeps. If there was rain, and there often was, the oaks seemed impervious. In a full sun, they rippled, like surf sparkling.

They had been there long before the runway was built, and would be there long after I left the base, went home, "rotated," as the military termed it. I remember hoping they'd be spared from being felled for another runway extension, or some sort of clotted housing estate development.

Sitting in that open-bay hut/barracks (where German POWs were housed in WWII, we discovered), looking off as those oaks danced slowly, I once wrote a twenty-two page letter to my sister back in the States. She never said much, though, in her subsequent letters about it, of my rambling rant about my "generation", how we were different. I often wondered if she'd saved it somewhere – I'd loved to have read it and met who I was then. Years later, in the middle of a dinner table conversation, she said, out of the famous blue, "That was some letter you wrote me – from England." I wanted to ask "What did I say?" But the moment passed as quickly as it came. And I never did ask her.

THE COLD WAR

So this is the way it went. The Goodie Wagon came about nine-fifteen. By then, you'd had the second or third Pall Mall, savoring it with fresh chow hall coffee out of a West Bend metal urn. Depth-charge coffee, Bombardier coffee.

"Black as hell...like oil sludge..." Tech Sergeant Forbes would say. "Those goddamn cooks! They'll kill us before the Russians do!"

Sergeant Forbes drank cup after cup after cup. As the day progressed, his face got redder and redder, and he sped about the office like a souped-up mini car. At noon he retired into the brightly lit recess of the Target Vault, an actual bank-like vault where Top Secret maps were kept. Here, among other activities, Sergeant Forbes read pornographic novels he obtained in

London, in Soho, the vast sink of iniquity south of the base.

One of the recent mysteries of the big air base in the Midlands of England was how a hedgehog had gotten into this vault. "Hedgy", he was called. An animal control specialist had been summoned from Cambridge, twenty miles away, to capture the creature.

"Lucky it ain't a possum. They can take your hand off in a minute. Ever see their teeth?" the Cajun said, baring his. Paul Ambrose. He nodded. "Make a good stew, possum..."

The Cajun was a short-timer, and did not give a shit, having served most of his three-year tour in Germany. Oil had been discovered on land his family owned, back in Louisiana, and he was, he claimed, assured of being "a rich motherfucker" when he got discharged in a couple months. He talked of little else. "You bet yer ass I ride in a Caddy *El Dorado*! Shit!"

Accordingly, and amazingly, the Cajun had already had two suits made for himself at a tailor's in Cambridge. Clad in one of these, a dark blue one – topped with a real bowler hat

– he went to London, mystifying the Brits on the train to Kings Cross. He drank from a forty-ouncer of *Johnnie Walker* en route, holding court in his compartment.

However, he could recall little of what actually transpired once he alighted in London. He could not even recall how he left Kings Cross station, nor how he returned to the base (probably the good offices of fellow airmen). He returned with his bespoke suit "broken in," as he put it.

"I saw this Frenchman down there, in a place we went. He ate a hamburger, man! With a knife and fork. Like this." He demonstrated.

But the bowler hat was gone.

UNDERGROUND

It had been after a terrible, long winter, an English winter. Only a Scottish winter was worse. He'd kept track of every day it rained, and after forty-four days straight, he stopped. But the rain continued. To top it off, the huge ancient boiler which drove the heating system in the barracks, the hot water in the showers, shut down. For ten days. So that year he badly wanted Spring to come.

Spring in England was famous – in high school he'd read Browning's famous poem, although for some reason it was Shelley's great ode, ending with " O, wind, if Winter comes, can Spring be far behind?" that went straight to the heart.

So when this long-awaited Spring finally came, he set in motion a project he'd dreamed of laying in the cold barracks at night, wrapped in his issue greatcoat, under the blankets. It would take some time. Take him into Spring, surely. Ride the London Underground as much as he could. Just *go*. Come up out of "the Tube," the Underground – and see how London – this famous place, this site, this *name* - looked in Spring. Persephone returning.

He started from Piccadilly Circus, the central most underground station, the Blue Line traversing the heart of the big city. (One legend had it that if you stood in Piccadilly Circus long enough, you'd meet somebody you knew.) From there, to Russell Square, Bloomsbury, the British Museum, wet streets, many flower boxes. A subtle green shading in the famous square's trees.

On to Barbican, really old London, Roman walls still there. 1950's architecture to replace the fire bombing of the Blitz of World War II, particularly heavy here. Not far away, Bunyan and Blake buried.

How many Springs in England? Why did you think of such idle questions, anyway? Were they idle?

He kept a log of the journey in a small blue journal he carried in his jacket pocket. The racketing noise of the Tube, an unmistakable sound once heard, gave him a rush of the great soccer clubs of the city. Arsenal Chelsea Tottenham Hotspurs West Ham Crystal Palace (lasted a hundred years, then burnt down) Aston Villa ("the Villa"). The fearsome Manchester United – "United! United!", the soccer hooligans' chant. Not a London team.

And it gave him the unforgettable ones. Elephant and Castle. Baker Street. St. John's Wood (Paul McCartney's first house, with his piano in it; he still lives there). Hampstead (the house in whose garden John Keats heard the nightingale). Knightsbridge. Marble Arch. Whitechapel. Sloane Square...

And, finally, all the way out - a whole April day in Kew Gardens. And then to Richmond. Richmond, where the Thames curves beautifully. Richmond, he found, than which there can be no better place to be in Spring.

NELSON'S COLUMN

A moment.

Sundays in London nothing happens. Church happens. The hugeness of St. Paul's, even in huge London. A church where John Donne preached. Dr. Donne.

By Sunday, if you were down on week-end from the air base, you were probably near broke, in any case. Enough for an awful *Wimpy* burger ("made of old sawdust"), and some poor, weak tea.

He walks to Trafalgar Square. So familiar it was hard to remember when it wasn't. And the big square is filling, rapidly, and Nelson's Column above it all, so visible. If a virgin passes, he'll come down – London folk lore. The square looks Hogarthian. The squalor, stinks, rush,

hubbub of 18th century London. Londinium...
Neal's Yard. Seven Dials, not far...

What is happening? A grey Sunday in
London, and somebody is at the far end of the
big square, up on a wooden platform, with a
microphone. The crowd is dense now, growing
by the second, so he hangs on the shifting edge,
as much as possible.

It is a speaker, agitated, in brown clothing,
arms moving, jerking. And now he sees the men
near him opening their jackets. Some pass a
bottle of whiskey, there is a strong odor of feral
sweat. Some men have short, thick clubs they
are half-concealing, but now touching, under
their bulky jackets. And this sight sends a jolt
through him. He has seen demonstrations –
"demos" – before here, but they're more likely
at Hyde Park Corner, where the tradition of
speakers is legendary. You can hear anything
there on a Sunday. The only forbidden speech
is denunciation of the Queen, the monarch, calls
for her removal.

The speaker has an unmistakable accent – it
is Irish, and he realizes this is some sort of Irish

Republican rally, and the clubs mean trouble. The men near him are red in the face, leaning, some crouching, clenched, and the speaker's voice is rising. He calls out "Down with the bloody Queen! Down! Down with her!" And the huge crowd moves, pitches, rolls, a squad of blue-clad bobbies is pulling the struggling speaker down, onto the platform, in a melee of scattering papers flying up like pigeons, the static scratching and booming of the PA system, now, by someone, thrown from the stage into the crowd.

The men near him have taken out the clubs, he hears the smash of glass, screams erupt, and he realizes what is happening, but feels unable to move.

Trying to turn, and get off the square, away, he feels pulled, pushed, every direction, shoved violently, even a blow in the back. The clubs... somebody has his arm, turning, he sees it's a young woman with wide eyes, who pulls hard on his arm.

"With me. Come with me..."

He staggers, nearly falls, shoving with

one hand, the woman pulling – don't let go – the noise is everywhere, a bad sound, and he wonders suddenly if he will fall. Fall, be trampled. He feels bodies pressing everywhere, and then, like a cork, he is pulled out of the thick wedge of people, running now behind the woman, still holding her hand, across the mad street, down, down the gritty stairs, into the Tube stop, and then down more steps, sound of the trains, peoples' faces a blur, but some kind of order.

And then on a platform, the familiar platform, seeing the familiar train coming, hearing it. But the girl is gone, he turns and sees her going into another platform entrance, looking back at him. A flash of face in the other faces. Gone. She had helped him, now left.

Standing in the rocketing train car rushing through the darkness under London, he is swaying, holding grimly onto a worn leather strap, wondering at how quickly it all has happened.

And at how still he felt.

DOWN IN DORSET

So you sit in this exquisite 17th century house, which has very small rooms because people *were* smaller then. The diet. They rarely ate meat, couldn't afford it; illegal to hunt, to poach. Or fish the stream running through. Set the mastiff on you, or crush you in the mantrap. You're expendable. A peasant.

The small rooms induce, though, some sort of restraint into your prose, and your work is getting shorter. Is that better? How many pages a day do you need – to pay up, cover it all, put some aside for the many, many rainy days to come, in Dorset? To walk the prehistoric Chesil Beach?

Looking at the pieces. The "drafts", the long queue on the flickering computer screen, at, what, 2am? Who's awake in Dorset, at 2am? In

Hardy's Dorchester? The Dorset Insomniac...

Here's one. On Emmett and his Danish Reading Pipe, he got it in Greenland. You can stuff enough aromatic baccy in the bowl for a long, long read in those Arctic Circle nights, your pipe your fireplace. But then – what? A brick, a kilo, of Jordanian hash?

Well, hell, all the books he read, and he read many. *Oblomov*, for one. That is a long novel about economy, really, the subject of all real Russian novels.

Here. This one. The girl who went to the Altamont Festival in a hearse. She was fourteen. Couldn't get too far on that one. A couple paragraphs. No frequency.

What's this one? "When I read the *New York Times Book Review* and the *New York Review of Books*, I feel like no book I'd ever write would be reviewed in these pages."

And some *real* fiction. Carlos Leon, sixty years old, found shot dead, at 9 in the morning, in a rooming house in the Excelsior District. Those in nearby rooms reported hearing him say, before he was shot, "May God forgive."

Another. An elderly woman, found dead on the floor in her house in an upscale community. None of her neighbors could recall seeing her in five years.

A third, and a fourth. Must make fiction from these.

In some way even he may not have intended, Richard Brautigan's advice, given years ago at a San Francisco streetcar boarding platform – to just make up things in a résumé – was liberating.

But liberation can have its pitfalls, its sudden rapids. And then the long, long plunging waterfall, the no-return.

ORDINARY HAPPINESS

1966. In those days we lived in a ramshackle, upstairs flat like you can't find anymore except in the movies, on 21st Street, overlooking the city. The house was owned by a wealthy man who also owned race horses, which he took much better care of than his houses. And he probably found nothing odd in this.

1966 was the peak of the Hippie revolution, which had followed hard on the heels of the notorious Beatniks. High tide, Ground Zero, San Francisco. Thousands of people came into the city daily, from everywhere on the planet. Some stayed a couple hours, some a couple days or months, or years. Some never left. It was all happening, right in the street, right in front of you. Hour by hour.

In the fresh morning I cut a small white rose out back in the wildly sloping garden, which seemed about to go downhill into the next street at any time. Put it in my suit or sports jacket lapel. Wear it to work.

In the Mens' Room, the Office Manager pointed to it. "What's that supposed to mean?" He told me not to wear any more to work, but I did, the next day, then the next. And I was fired.

That was The Sixties.

POT

After the long, long harsh winter in (maybe) March, some hint of softness came in the air. Out in the unpaved street – really an alley – in this "lower end" of town, the first sign of Spring is playing Pot – shooting colored marbles into a small hole, the "pot," dug in the nearly soft ground. A player takes as many marbles as he can drive into this pot with their own marble – the shooter's marble – as long as it doesn't go into the pot also.

Pot is even before baseball in marking Spring, when dusty gloves are dug out, oiled carefully – or, if one is very fortunate, a new glove purchased, than which *nothing* could be better.

The ground around the pot could be smoothed out, all small stones, pebbles, thrown away. But it would still be a rough, challenging surface to shoot on. In making a shot, the shooter had to calculate this surface carefully – the drag, the slope of it, any incidental small shadow-like declivities that could deflect or hang up a shot. Although none of us knew anything of golf - greens, putting – the resemblances, the slow scrutiny and study of the ground surface, was similar. We were more familiar with the resemblance to pool, played uptown in the infamous Schaeffer's Pool Hall, where none of us were supposed to go, or enter.

The marbles themselves were small marvels of bright colors smaller kids had been known to try to eat, thinking them candy. A full sack of them meant a good season played, a certain respect. One could spread them out over a table, and admire them there, like stars. They were in the realm of a good collection of comic books.

The skill involved in making shots which banked, hooked, ricocheted one or more marbles into the pot, was admired. Some shot using the thumb; some the forefinger, or the longer second finger, after carefully sighting, which could require even l ying on the ground. Thus the mothers' refrain; "How can you get so dirty playing marbles?"

Why marbles, the game of Pot, were particularly linked to the coming of Spring nobody could say. It just was. That was the way things were. Nobody played Pot at any other time of the year. Baseball would start up almost simultaneously, the first thrill of the sound of somebody playing catch, that familiar, satisfying smack of the ball in a glove. Old Mr. Saunders, whose house sat on one side of the alley-street where we played Pot, and later very loud and often very long pick-up games of baseball, would be seen peering sharply out of his front window, which had been broken before by hit or thrown balls, boys scattering simultaneously in all directions, while he emerged, red-faced, shaking his cane, yelling "You goddamn kids!"

But that – baseball – that was Summer.

KINGDOM OF DUMPLING

P enny Lane was named that by her parents, in 1968. They had been at the last live Beatles concert in Candlestick Park in San Francisco on August 21, 1966.

Back in the day, as they say...but now it was now, right now. The here and now And Penny's older brother, Joop, was driving the blue Subaru. The morning coffee foray. To the Velo Rouge, for the fabled Blue Bottle coffee. But the place is closed. A fire. Late Friday night, 11:30 or so, water heater. Son of a bitch.

There was nothing for it but to go to the fall-back, Ritual Coffee, runner-up to Blue Bottle. That meant a safari, down into The Mission.

So. Down to Valencia Street. It was 11 am and the hipsters were not out and about quite yet, but a guy went by with a long pole carried on his shoulder, holding multi-colored shirts, vests, skirts, and one yellow and red hat, which looked like a parrot. The sun was all over the place, and there was a lot of parking, an oddity.

"There was an earthquake," Joop, driving with his usual dodgum-cars style, said, as if in explanation. "At 4:33 am..."

"Terra incognita," he said, gesturing around him with stretched out arms wide, as we walked from the neatly parked car. "Yeah... used to be shops down here they sold used military footlockers, old steamer trunks. People used them for tables...also, those phone cable spools, big mothers...Now look at it."

Pregnant words. You could go around the world in two blocks. There was a Pakistani-Indian place, a zinc-fronted bar called Zeitgeist, a "Peruvian," Limon, a *taqueria*, a pizzeria, the all-American Bi-Rite Creamery right around the corner, not far from "the shrine where there's always a line," Tartine. And Bar Tartine, too.

That water heater fire at Velo Rouge. Sends us to Valencia Street, gleaming with *Bauhaus* condos in the full sun, across the street from Ritual Coffee, where we stood looking.

But we ended up in Asia. Out in the fog in the Sunset. Far out on Taraval, at Kingdom of Dumpling, a Harbin domain. While we ate those big dumplings, Joop talked of his summer travel plans.

"Go to Puebla and Oaxaca," he said.

A MOOSE IN
CARMEL

There are no moose in Carmel. My friend in Anchorage writes of seeing a starved, emaciated one in early April, gnawing at the tree bark in his driveway – starved for protein, which it will be able to get in just a week or so when the tree buds out, the tender bright green shoots. How good that must taste!

Robinson Jeffers built a stone house, stone by stone, himself (along with some help from friends), before World War One, in Carmel. The town developed as an artist colony, an idea of that time that, like nudism, wearing sandals, vegetarianism, and various types of socialism, was all the rage.

A recent survey of the four thousand plus

residents of Carmel revealed that about half of them list their residence there as a second home – or maybe a third, or fourth, or fifth. (Didn't the Enron guy have about fourteen? And didn't he have to sell off seven?) Many of these second homes sell for a few million, give or take a couple of hundred thou.

But no moose.

Unless you were in Maine. Thoreau wrote an entire book, *The Maine Woods*, which details the many moose in Maine in those days, and how to hunt them. And Thoreau had only one house, which he built himself, and then left after two and half years. This is the quilt of American experience.

There was a television sitcom, *Northern Exposure*, that began with a lonely moose walking down the main street of this small town in Alaska, where there are still many moose (moose is one of those English words that does not change to form the plural, driving learners of the language to distraction and anger). And so it was not unusual, what my friend saw.

But it would be unusual to see a moose in

Carmel. Despite all the houses, the lush gardens and lawns, no place to live.

But, there are many poodles in Carmel. Especially for the annual Poodle Day Parade. So. It's not unusual to see a poodle, or two, or even three. Even the rarely seen, very big Royals. In Carmel.

THE CLEAN AND THE DIRTY

There was a song that year, George Hamilton IV singing "A White Sport Coat and a Pink Carnation." But the desired look for young men was the Ivy League look. Rich, colorful, patterned shirts with the button-down collar. Chinos with a small buckle in back. And white bucks. These were critical.

On the latter, in particular, there was a sharp stylistic divide. (No one knew then of semantics and signifiers, it was hard to decipher past a point.) No, the issue, the big style question you had to wrestle with was - *clean* or *dirty* bucks? To err in this was serious, a matter for ostracism. (Girls did not have to worry about this. They wore two-toned saddle shoes.)

So at the high school, it was the *clean* look, the more pristine, the whiter, the better. Nobody knew why, he carefully asked around, but nobody knew. It just was. In the crowded halls, it took some doing, keeping them white. There was a cleaning brush, and white buck powder to remove or at least cover marks, scuffs, and stains. The latter could also be rectified with a white liquid, like typewriter white-out, applied with a small brush and let dry. But beyond a certain point bucks were not salvageable. And there were the malevolent few in the halls who seemed determined to ruin them. That meant a new pair.

Those fortunate enough to go to a dirty white bucks institution – the big AA school down the road, for example – had a far easier, more natural path, less military. And these same people also allowed rumpled chinos (but they had to have cuffs). They joined in the required wearing of V-neck sweaters, best with a blazing white tee-shirt underneath. A letter sweater, a cardigan, was ok, even without a *bona fide* letter, as long as there was the Ivy League shirt. The Ivy League look was, after all, collegiate.

It was also the only look that sanctioned glasses, which he'd worn since eighth grade. Heavy horn-rims were the preferred type. Worn with a crew-cut, this was definitely acceptable, definitely collegiate. He had seen, while riding by on the trolley, the frat men lounging out on the porch of their house at Carnegie Tech looking like this.

White bucks became comfortable the longer they were worn. but because even in the "dirty" style their longevity was apparent, they weren't footwear to be kept that long. Maybe two years, at most. They were "in," but at some point, overnight it seemed, they would be "out." Before them had been the heavy engineer boots (favored by the "greasers"), and before those, oxblood spade-toed/tipped shoes. And for one unforgettable year, blue suede shoes.

Yes. Blue suede shoes. You couldn't wear them in the rain. But somehow, even then, he knew they were a thousand miles from white bucks.

1967

Now all the professors look like 1967. Plaid lumberjack shirts, desert boots, no ties. Definitely, no ties. A few even sport suspenders.

In forty-odd years, the face of Academia so radically changed that if someone who left it at that time were to return, they would indeed be astounded. What would they make of it?

1967 was maybe the last whole year of a type of collegiate experience now as remote as the Revolutionary War. Earlier in that tumultuous decade, in December of 1963, on the campus at UC Berkeley, the *Free Speech Movement* had its triumphs, and its publicity success. In an expression to become proverbial, the whole world was watching. The beginning of the Social Network, but nobody knew that then –

although some of course, today, claim they did. "Well, if you recall, I published an article about that time, and in that piece I specifically called attention..." Yes.

Everybody wanted to be a professor in those days. Or play in a newly formed rock band. The best student in my Chaucer class did the latter, and riding on the *M* car from the college he told me "You should look into it...it's going to be the thing."

I rode around San Francisco in my Belgian friend's Corvair, and we saw a lot of things. The radio blared away. " Light My Fire" came on. "Have you heard this?" my friend asked with his Belgian/French accent, his eyes wide. "It's unbelievable. Unbelievable. UN-be-liev-able!"

I had on a red Paisley cravat, a real cravat, bought at a shop in Cambridge, England. The windows of the beige Corvair were down, the air was hitting us, and I thought "I could wear this anywhere now."

Anywhere.

NEANDERTHAL

The Geography book was larger than the other class books, big for a third grade book, and this was to accommodate the many bright, colored maps. He loved these, and already wondered if he could be a geographer, and what it was they did? He had asked his mother, who said "You never know..." and smiled, which always made him feel better.

In the Geography book there was also a black and white drawing of a man, a Neanderthal man. Miss Matson, their teacher, who wore small, round, metal-framed glasses, said there were no longer any of these on Earth.

The man in the drawing was naked, and he pointed this out to Becky Foster, who sat across from him. She laughed, and would not look at the drawing that he pointed at. Then, the next day, he showed it to Nancy Harris, whose family was supposed to be rich, and were said to live in the most expensive house in the area, costing thirty thousand dollars, a sum he could not imagine. She smiled, but didn't laugh.

Two days later, as he again leaned over to point out the naked man to Becky Foster, who was also leaning toward him, Miss Matson, who was – how did she get there? – behind him, said "That's enough." She took him into the hallway, and told him he was not to "do that" anymore, that he knew what she meant, he was a smart boy, and that she would give him a note which he was not to read, but to give to his mother.

The high-ceilinged classroom was very quiet for the rest of the day. At three school ended, and he, as Miss Matson had said, received a small envelope, sealed, with his mother's name written on it. He was told "Don't open this."

He did not. He walked home quickly, his heart thumping so that he worried. What was in Miss Matson's note to his mother? Something about the naked man, whose hairy, dark image stuck in his brain. But what had he done?

As soon as he got in the door at the house, he gave his mother the small white envelope.

"From Miss Matson," he said. "I didn't open it."

She nodded, and he followed her into the small kitchen, where he stood by the table as she carefully opened the envelope, and took out a small white sheet of paper with ink handwriting on it. One side was covered with writing, and some was on the other, he could see, as his mother turned it over, reading. Then she looked at him.

"Miss Matson gave this to you?"

He nodded. He wanted to speak, but his throat was too dry, and he instead swallowed.

His mother smiled at him. And then, with a smooth gesture, she tore the note in two, and threw the pieces into the small garbage bin under the sink.

SMALL YELLOW PLASTIC ASHTRAY

I had met a rich girl the year before. Rich girls change your life. When I visited her in Manhattan, and took a cab from the Park Avenue apartment, the cabbie asked, checking me out in the rear view mirror, "You gonna marry that girl? Because let me tell you, you oughta."

I didn't marry her. Maybe my whole life would have been different, you know? That story? This is what happened instead.

It's Autumn 1967. Another time. And another place.

I carry a small, yellow plastic ashtray in my new tan leather briefcase. You can smoke in the classroom in college, and now, as the teacher, the first ritual I perform, to open the door for us all, is to set my briefcase (it has my three initials monogrammed on the lock flap) down on the square, scarred and rather small wooden desk at the front of the classroom, take out that small, yellow plastic ashtray (which has a brown-black, shaded burn mark on one side, where the cleverly placed slot to hold your burning cigarette is), take out my Tareytons, tap one expertly out – just one – get my Zippo from my tight, grey bell-bottomed corduroy pants pocket, flick it smoothly open, thumb it to light, and take a drag. Smooth, smooth.

"How are you today?" I say, and they speak — there is the susurrus of their voices. Somebody, or two or three, raise their hands, one or two scurry in late and slide into their desks, more than a few are lighting cigarettes now. So I can see what brands, with what kids. Camels – whoa! A cough already, no doubt, and a coffee, black drinker, through the night. Winstons – sorority girl, maybe. Kools. Old-fashioned, parents' brand. Pall Malls. Definitely a smoker. Kents. Health-conscious, maybe even an athlete. Chesterfields! Didn't know they were still around. Tareytons – sure enough, two, three.

There is a feeling in the room that's hard to describe (that oft-used, true phrase). A softness. A gentle tentativeness. Is this, here, now, us – real? And what are we really doing? Isn't it supposed to be an English class? Are we – can we even say it to ourselves – on the point of making some kind of crazy love? Is this skinny guy with Buddy Holly horn rims and low slung bell bottom corduroy trousers and a black sweater, wearing – no less – blue-green Indian love beads? Is he real? How did he come to be *here*? With us? And why? And what does it all mean?

Maureen. Cute, maybe nineteen, Catholic, a Cubbie fan from way back, will be a great wife, mother. Smiles right to the left ventricle. Linda. Shows me Jimi Hendrix album and gets me to dance to "Are You Experienced?", which causes so much noise two other teachers leave their classes to look in the door. The students beckon to them to come in. One complains, apparently. Kurt. Solid gold All-American, getting smarter every second of every day. But then, there is

Vietnam. Mary. Mary. Mary. Large blue eyes in the next to last row, the first one I look for but without showing it, but she knows. I fall into those eyes. She looks down at the floor.

This is what I will talk about today, what we will talk about. "Le Déjeuner des Canotiers," Auguste Renoir's painting; the young men in their white undershirts and summer straw hats, the young women looking intently at them, many bottles of wine everywhere. I ask them to imagine it as a still – then it comes to life, as the beginning of a film. A Truffaut-like film. A great idea for the opening, the establishing shot, maybe we will return to it periodically as the film progresses.

Then – as always – the class comes to an end, But reluctantly. They crowd close in around that old beat-up desk; one sits on it. "Want to know how many cigarettes you smoked today? I'll tell you. Seven. Seven!" I will drink a half-pint of Christian Brothers later, after I eat a plate of spaghetti in my upstairs flat in a wooden frame house right off the campus that has already-vintage rock show posters from the Fillmore on the walls and a very large poster of D H Lawrence looking right at you (we are reading *Sons and Lovers*) and record albums on wooden shelves on cement blocks and many, many books (most paperback), and an old Victorian-style sofa with an elegantly curved back, upholstered in dark green. And a light on at 4 am most mornings, if you happen to pass by.

That class. That one. Wherever you are. *Section 72, '67*. Has never ended. I want to get that down. There.

PARIS, 1959

1

Paris, pearl-grey and white, Christmas 1959. Arriving by train, gliding into the *Gare du Nord*, past the *Sacré-Cœur*, The *Hôtel de Flore*, Left Bank, up a steep, winding hill. Big tub at the end of the hall, the young maid asking "Vous lavez?" Smoky existentialist cellar, "Le Cave St. Germain", all the rage. Boul Mich. A very young Brigitte Bardot, being filmed with hand-held camera, (Raoul Coutard?) right in the café across from the church. James Jones still living in style on the *Île de la Cité*, but soon to return from exile to Long Island.

Rain, ten days, the streets a constant amazement, like being in a painting.

2

It is a minute or two past midnight. Devotion is a small town.

The Trailways bus, sitting in the soft darkness, smoking Tareytons, the darkened bus running up through the middle of Pennsylvania, where there is a larger terminal, Dubois, famous for deer hunting. Point of transfer. Then, the run into the upper reaches of the Appalachians, now worn down, rounded dark ridges along the road, slipping by silently.

Into the town you live in, surprised to feel the warmth, the sense of being home. It is five am on an early September morning, the sky now lightening, and the bus driver leaves you off near where you live, the big door making that unmistakable bus door sound as it opens and closes.

Step into quiet, almost a hush. A pause. Summer warmth still in the air, but a slight hint of something else, coming. Only a random car or two, none on the side streets. A light or two on, here and there, in houses. The town is green with large trees, lawns. White frame houses, lived in, and that certain oldness of Eastern towns. A church, built in 1792...

This is the place. But you will have to leave it.

MAIL BOX

Philip Guston would have painted this faded-in-shades blue US Postal Service mail box, a species going extinct. The secret is to see it. To see it stolid, alone, waiting for its entire existence on an empty street with no cars – *no cars* – parked near it or in front of it. One street lamp, standing sentinel.

It helps if the sky is huge high blue with large clouds easily moving. The mail box and sky. The same rich colors, impossible to wear out. If you can imagine it, you can see it. It.

The mail box has received all manner of communications, dreams, wishes, hopes, in its years of ultimate patience and security. Why has no one unbolted it, in the middle of the night, taken it away? Sat it in a living room, to look at it?

It is not lonely, somehow. But it has known loneliness.

If only Guston could've painted it. The perfect, spiritual, mail box. Blue's essence.

Maybe he did.

DEEP SOUND

The fog horns, unmistakable, always send a small shiver up the spine. The old, rotting docks creak. A body, some crabs still at it, snagged, hoisted with a whoosh, by an uncomprehending fisherman. Longshoremen in an all-night Edward Hopper café. The rattle of dice, slammed on the bar. Jameson Irish in a small hip flask. Amber in the shot glass. Wet neon streets, cold. Pea jacket, watch cap, black leather gloves. Jack London and the oyster pirates of Sausalito. Hammett, his tailored grey overcoat collar up, coming out of John's Grill, looks up the street. Kerouac, standing smoking a cigarette, outside Vesuvio's. Bob Kaufman, silent for ten years. Lying by the flickering, warm fireplace, hearing those foghorns moan outside.

Walking home, two am, they keep you company, while the fog spins in front of you like a Sufi dervish, the deep lessons of the desert.

THE CAFÉ CHAIR

Made of curved smooth metal so it would not break if used in a riot. Not the most comfortable chair. But the patron doesn't want comfort, but money, so no one should sit too long, dawdling over a single glass or cup. "You want another?" at 3am.

The seat is smooth very faded stained leather, stretched like a drum head. How many asses' friction would it take to engineer such a glassy surface? If it (the seat) could speak, indeed there would be stories.

The chairs sit like military formations, ranks awaiting orders. Late at night, there is a forlorn melancholy – is it the artificial lighting? – in their emptiness, their profound patience. They have been made to perform only one function, and they await that.

The noise of the classic café chair being drawn back to sit is unmistakable, and ugly. An odd fact, that. In many, many cases, the sitting about to occur, the putting of a lead-heavy ass on that seat, is really desired. A focused, full act. So too the drawing back of the chair, prior to standing. Leaving. The dancing shadows of the leaves of nearby trees, if one is lucky, pattern the table. One could look forever.

At some point, the chair is retired. Perhaps sold for scrap, even, ignominious. But it may be bought in an odd lot by an antiques dealer, re-sold to a shop, finally purchased by a young woman decorating her apartment in some city. She takes it home, with some difficulty, on a bus, attracting a variety of looks, and installs it in her small entrance hall, where its presence is duly and often noted, in passing. Coats, scarves, hats, bags are placed on it. Draped, hung, piled carelessly.

Once in a while all this detritus is cleared, and it stands alone, only itself, complete, needing nothing. Something else, full of stories it cannot tell, but only summon.

Small architecture.

TEA

His blood pressure was going down. The lower, the better. He was drinking more tea, and not only that, but it was tea from France, from Mariage Frères, and Harney's. The French had the best tea in the world, but no one knew it. Just as they had the best hot chocolate, but no one believed that, either. The French drink wine! Everybody knew that.

There had been a place in Paris when they were there. Maybe up in the Marais. As they walked by they'd seen an old, white-bearded man hunched over a small journal, writing, with a cigarette in one hand, the smoke curling up. A striking-looking face, even through the window. He could have been a veteran of the Maquis, in World War II. What was he writing? Was he waiting for a friend to join him? The ubiquitous small white cup and saucer were at his elbow. But he did not drink. The smoke from the cigarette curled up into his face, and he squinted at the white page in front of him, bending closer, intent.

Thinking of this made him want to see *My Dinner with Andre*. Now that was a film about New York. Made by a Frenchman. His wife seriously disliked it.

"The most boring film ever made. It's as bad, if not worse, than *One Hundred Years of Solitude*, the most boring novel ever written."

In *My Dinner with Andre*, he was pretty sure the old waiter, a marvelous character who never spoke, served them coffee.

Of course, there was also John-Pierre Melville's *Army of Shadows*. But that – that was another story.

THE WORK

They went out back and smoked; another garbage-strewn rat alley. The Loop Lounge, Cleveland. The set: "Lush Life", "Stella by Starlight," "It Never Entered My Mind," "My Funny Valentine," "Yesterdays."

"Lots of ballads...", the piano player said. The moon slipped out overhead, between two buildings.

"Yeah...it's the last set. I like ballads." the trumpet player said. "Get lost in them." He was thinking of a girl in Los Angeles. Her hair was like smoke in autumn, and cognac. "Write one like that," she'd said. "You can do it. For me."

The bassist nodded, stretched, looked up. "Stars up there," he said, pointing with a long fingered hand.

The piano player put his coat collar up. "We were playing in KC once, it got so quiet, and somebody went outside, in the back there, and it was snowing." He nodded. "It had a sound – I don't know what it was, but snow sounds. Like smoke curls up, from an ashtray?"

"Yeah," the trumpet player said. "Yeah..."

"And I thought, damndest thing, I thought about playing the piano in snow, snow falling around me, like. A piano player in snow. Bass man in snow. Drummer. The whole quartet, you know?"

They were all looking at him, grouped in their small circle there, like they did on stage. The piano player looked tired in the harsh overhead night lighting of the next door building.

"How come piano players always look tired?" the trumpet player asked.

The piano player shrugged, looked down, shook his head, said nothing.

"Cleveland...hey, what was that place, in Italy?" The bass player pointed at them, with his large right hand. "Lucca? Something like that..." Then he pointed up, towards the sliver of dark sky.

"Guy here last night. Out back here. He threw a whiskey bottle - empty – over top that brick building right there. Three stories. Heard it smash on the other side."

The trumpet player smiled. "Strozzapreti. Strangle the priest. The pasta, in Italy, in Lucca. Remember?"

"Cold here in winter," the drummer said. He hadn't spoken. He hunched his shoulders. "Cold. That wind, off the lake..."

They all involuntarily shivered, looked around, nodded, and filed back in the green-black rusted back door of The Loop Lounge.

BEFORE THE INTERNET

Walking late at night in snowy street of small town –some snow falling. A sense of calm, peacefulness.

Mailing a letter, in front of the grey stone post office building, with a statue of a Civil War soldier in front.

THE OLD GUY

The old guy – he was seventy-one – lived in a houseboat in the far end of Sausalito. He wrote *haiku*, and walked his dog, very late at night, even early morning; say, two or two-thirty am (maybe he wrote *haiku* then, too.) At that time, Sausalito reverts to a very small town. Nothing is open except three small hotel lobbies, and a few stragglers hang around outside Bill's, a funky toilet of a bar on Caledonia. All more or less drunk. Mostly more.

I followed him around for a while ...one of his friends was a painter who actually lived in the Industrial Center Building, the famous ICB where Liberty Ships were built during WWII, one every thirty days at the height of it, but never admitted as much, since it was illegal. They'd go for coffee together, at Fish or up the street, at Fred's, or the new place, Cibo.

Bill's, though, is the kind of bar where guys still "go outside" to fight. "Did you ever have a fistfight?" a girl once asked me, truly out of the famous blue. "No..." I haltingly answered.

"I didn't think so," she said. A great, masterful, crushing put-down, almost British in its force and sharpness. But I had been in a fistfight, in grade school, when in a fit of rage I'd punched the other boy hard as I could directly on his nose, and blood had sprayed out directly on my shirt, and I had burst into tears.

JASS

Around Piccadilly Circus and Soho there were all manner of things. Anything was possible. In Wardour and Greek Streets, bill boards displayed 3x5 cards advertising the various services of "French" maids and skilled *masseuse*; a woman "from Hamburg" and several from Berlin. Mona, from Hong Kong.

He and Ambrose walked, and walked some more. Ambrose was a driver in the Base Motor Pool, so good that he'd been selected to drive the Wing Commander's car – Colonel Frost. As such, he had experience driving in London.

"The driving on the left stuff – took some getting used to. It still doesn't feel right, you know? Why the hell do they do it?"

"Search me...I hear they do the same in

Sweden."

Ambrose stopped to light a cigarette. He drew heavily on it, and looked at it appreciatively. "You can't get a good smoke here, either..."

"What about the Jamaicans?"

He nodded, smiling. "That's true. Northampton's good. Guy up there, takes a joint outta his trouser cuff! I saw that...outside this pub."

It seemed like the streets in London were always wet. They were looking for some place that had jazz – modern jazz. A jazz club. They had found, on previous expeditions, Ronnie Scott's, but it was somewhat expensive. There were a number of places that had "trad," which many British favored. It was "traditional jazz," which meant Dixieland. He had heard arguments in coffee bars in Soho that Dixieland, "trad" was the real, original, authentic "jass" - which was the original term, not jazz.

They had found one place, where you paid a membership. The club, called The Green Door, being Members Only, could thus get around the pub licensing hours rule, and serve after eleven pm. Then there was a cellar club, La Rocca's, where you could hear flamenco and classical guitar. People sat quietly, many wearing sunglasses, although it was night. It was the style.

On this night, they rounded a corner, not far from Piccadilly, and heard what sounded like jazz. Ambrose grabbed his arm.

"Hear that?"

He nodded. While they stood listening, a man stopped in front of them.

"You looking for girls?" He smiled knowingly.

"No," Ambrose said curtly.

The man raised his hands in front of himself, and then was gone, into the flow of pedestrians.

"It's coming from up there..."Ambrose pointed to a square of yellow light, a window on the second floor of a building a few doors down the narrow street.

When they got to the street level doorway, they saw a small sign jutting out above the door. It read "Club Afrique". A steep flight of stairs led up to what looked like a closed door.

"Some kind of African joint...never run into

one of these down here before."

"There's everything in London," Ambrose said. "Let's go up, see what it is. It sounds good."

It was a steep climb up to the heavy-looking, dark wooden door. There was a small peephole in the upper center of the door.

"Like those speakeasy doors," Ambrose said. He shrugged. "What the hell." He rapped sharply on the big door; they waited, hearing the muffled sounds of what was definitely interesting, live music. There was no response. Ambrose pounded with his closed fist, harder, and they saw an eye at the peephole. Then the door opened.

A very large, tall man stood completely blocking the doorway. He was dark, a blackness of a powerful depth and intensity, an almost blue-blackness. This man was completely bald, and wore a grey turtleneck sweater.

"What you want?" he asked, looking from one of them to the other, folding his arms in front of his massive chest. Both of them had moved involuntarily slightly back from the doorway.

Ambrose made a slight gesture with his head. "We want to come in – listen to the music? We could hear it, outside." He pointed back down the stairs. "We like jazz..."

The man said nothing, looking intently at them. Then he shook his head. "This the *Club Afrique*, mon. This club for Africans." With that, he shut the heavy door with a thud.

They turned and went carefully back down the narrow, steep stairs. It would be a bad business to be thrown down those stairs.

Outside, it was that soft rain of London, and the wet streets of Soho glinted around them.